Agapanthus Hum and Major Bark

Joy Cowley
author of Mrs. Wishy-Washy
Pictures by Jennifer Plecas

PHILOMEL BOOKS • NEW YORK

PATRICIA LEE GAUCH, EDITOR.

Philomel Books, Reg. U.S. Pat. & Tm. Off. Published simultaneously in Canada.
Printed in Hong Kong by South China Printing Co. (1988) Ltd.
Book design by Sharon Murray Jacobs. The text is set in 17-point Goudy Old Style.
Library of Congress Cataloging-in-Publication Data
Cowley, Joy. Agapanthus Hum and Major Bark / Joy Cowley ; pictures by Jennifer Plecas. p. cm.
Summary: After Agapanthus gets a puppy for a pet,
she enters him in a champion dog show and comes away with a surprising result.
[1. Dogs—Fiction.] I. Plecas, Jennifer, ill. II. Title.
PZ7.C8375 Ad 2001
[E]—dc21 98-4897
ISBN 0-399-23322-9
1 3 5 7 9 10 8 6 4 2
First Impression

Table of Contents

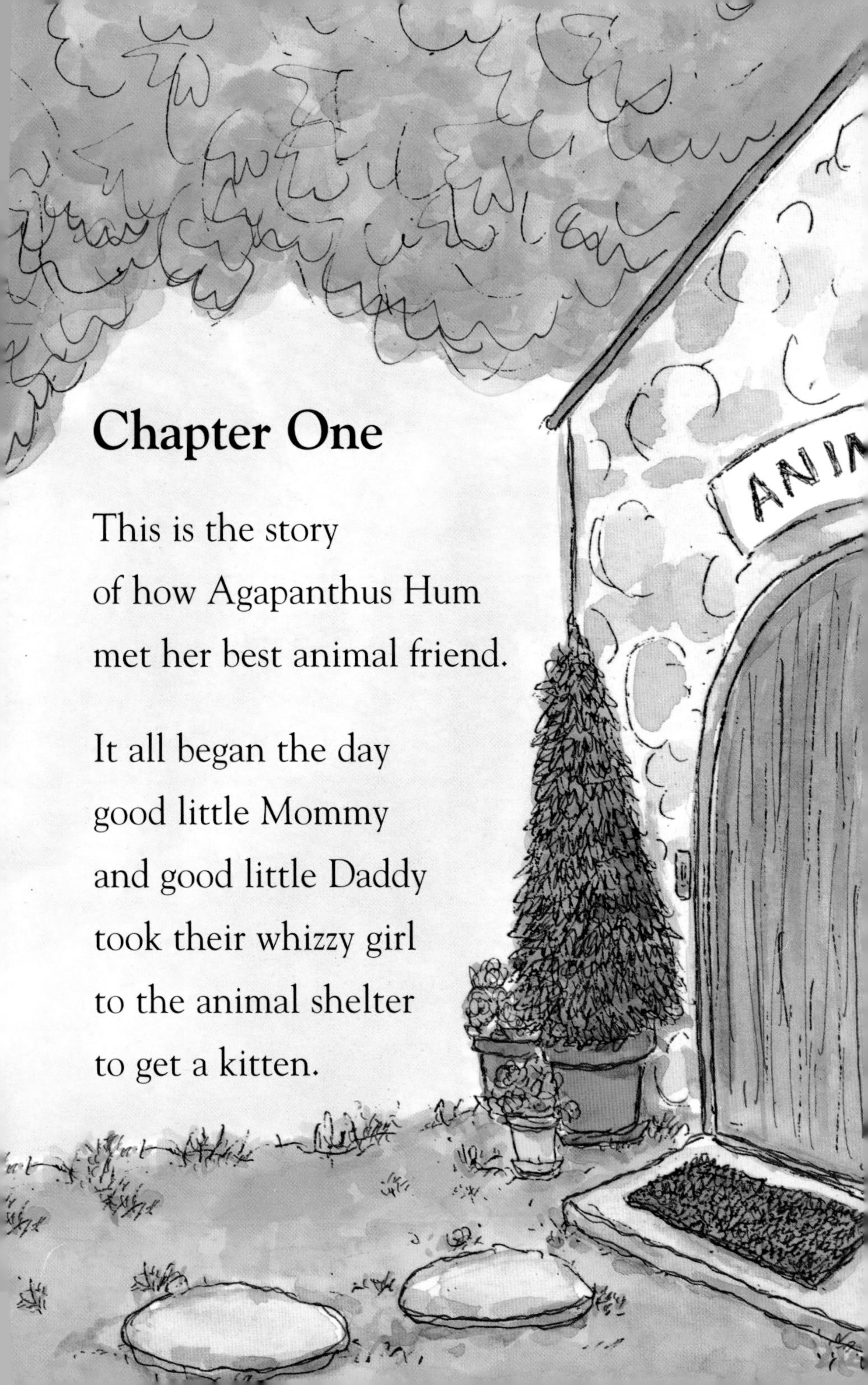

Chapter One

This is the story
of how Agapanthus Hum
met her best animal friend.

It all began the day
good little Mommy
and good little Daddy
took their whizzy girl
to the animal shelter
to get a kitten.

They saw black-and-white kittens,
ginger kittens, gray kittens,
kittens with purrs,
and kittens with sticky claws.

They also saw a little dog
with floppy ears, short legs,
and a tail like electric string.

When Agapanthus picked up
a fluffy ginger kitten,
the dog lay on his back
and whined.

Agapanthus stroked
the ginger kitten.
The dog waggled his paws
and squeaked at her.

Good little Daddy said, "Honey,
is that the kitten
you like best?"

Agapanthus put down
the ginger kitten.
She did not want to tell
good little Daddy
that she liked the dog best.

She turned around
and put her hand
in the dog's cage.
The dog squeaked and
squeaked and licked
her fingers.

"Darling," said good little Mommy,
"we have no room for a dog."

"We had planned for a kitten,"
said good little Daddy.

But the heart of Agapanthus Hum
was so full of squeaky little dog
that there was no space left over
for a kitten of any kind.
She put her face against the dog's cage.
The dog whined and shivered
and licked her glasses
right off her eyes.

“Oh, dear!” cried her mother,
grabbing the glasses.

“He kissed me!” Agapanthus laughed.
“He wants me to take him home!”

Good little Mommy
and good little Daddy
looked at each other.
“Well,” said good little Daddy,
“it seems like we’ve got us a dog.”

Chapter Two

A hum fizzed in Agapanthus
like cherry soda pop
as she cuddled the little dog
in the back of the car.
“What kind of dog is he?”
she asked good little Daddy.

"Let me see," he said.
"His body is like a zucchini.
His legs are like celery sticks.
His tail is a string bean,
and his ears are lettuce leaves.
I guess that makes him a salad."

"No! Really!" laughed Agapanthus.

Good little Mommy said,
"This is a bitser dog.
He has many breeds in him.
A bit of this. A bit of that."

Agapanthus said to the dog,
"Bitser, we will have to think
of a very good name for you."

The dog had grown tired
of squeaking and bouncing.
He lay in Agapanthus's
lap and closed his eyes.

Agapanthus felt as though
she had swallowed
the biggest smile in the world.
The fizzy tune in her head
suddenly hummed out
through her nose.
The little dog jumped up,
his eyes wide open.
This time he did not squeak.
He barked. *Wuff-wuff-wuff!*

Agapanthus laughed.
"My hum!" she said to the dog.
"It woke you up and made you bark."

"Now there's a fine name
for a fine bitser dog,"
said good little Mommy.
"Major Bark. Major, for short."

Chapter Three

There were times
when the arms and legs
of Agapanthus Hum
did whizzy things
all by themselves.

But Major Bark was whizzy
morning, noon, and night.

While he
was asleep,
his paws scrabbled
and his nose
twitched
with dreaming.

When he was awake,
he did a whole lot of
chewing.
He growled at socks
and shook them
into holes.
He bit pieces
out of shoes.

"He is still a puppy,"
said good little Daddy.
"He is cutting
his teeth."

Major loved
to bite anything
that belonged to
Agapanthus Hum.

If she left her clothes
lying on the floor,
he would
find them.

“My T-shirt!”
she cried.
“It’s got slobber
and holes!”

“He likes your smell
because he thinks
you belong to him,”
said good little
Mommy.

“He will grow out of it.
Look at it this way:
He is helping you
to learn to be tidy.”

Agapanthus was quiet
for the longest time.
Then she said, “Oh, pickles!”

Chapter Four

Agapanthus's friends loved Major.
They came over every day
to play with him.

"He is very clever," said Taylor,
throwing him her tennis ball.
"Look at the way he can catch!"

Major brought the ball back,
and Taylor took it from him.
"It is all wet!" She laughed.
"That is so cute!"

Major loved to show off
in front of the children.
He ran in circles,
chasing his tail
and yapping
like a firecracker.

He wobbled on
his back legs
to beg for bits of cookie.

Orville reckoned that Major
was the best dog in town.
"He's great. He's smart.
Why don't you enter him
in the Champion Dog Show?"

"You must!" cried Taylor.
"Major would absolutely win."

Agapanthus put her arms
around Major Bark.
She shut her eyes
as he licked her glasses.
"I'll think about it,"
she said.

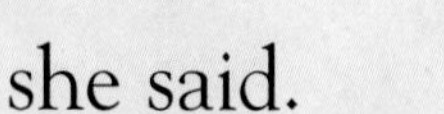

Chapter Five

Good little Mommy
tried to explain:
"Dog shows are not for dogs
like Major Bark," she said.
"He is not one pure breed
like a pedigree collie
or cocker spaniel."

"He is a champion bitser,"
said Agapanthus Hum.
"People love him
the way he is."

“I know, I know,”
said good little Mommy.
“He is quite wonderful,
and we love him, too.
But I don’t think that bitsers
are allowed in the dog show.”

Good little Daddy
smiled at Agapanthus.
“Honey, we think you
will be very disappointed.
But if you really want Major
to go to that flea circus,
then okay, you can take him.”

Chapter Six

The dogs and their owners
stood all around
the show grounds.
There were big dogs
and little dogs,
dogs with long hair,
dogs with curly hair, and
dogs with haircuts.

Major Bark did not like
his new collar and lead,
but he was very excited
to see so many dogs.
He shivered all over
and squeaked like a rusty gate.

Agapanthus tried to hold him,
but he shook his head
until it slid right out
of his collar. Then,
as quick as a tail wag,
he ran away to yip hello
to a bulldog.

All the other dogs joined in.
Some dogs pulled away
from their owners
and bounded around the ring,
sniffing and licking, yapping
and woofing, tumbling in a heap
around Major Bark.

Owners called out commands
like "Sit!" and "Come!"
but the dogs took no notice.
Their barking grew as loud as
a full brass band.

At last Agapanthus Hum
got hold of Major Bark.
She held him tight
while he wriggled
and kissed her glasses.
He looked very pleased
with himself.

"Is this your
dog?" said the judge.

"Yes, ma'am!"
said Agapanthus.

"His name is
Major Bark.
He is a bitser."

"Really?" said the judge.

"A champion bitser,"
said Agapanthus Hum.

"I see," replied the judge,
smiling at Major Bark.
"Well, put his collar back on
and keep him with you
until we have finished
this part of the judging."

Chapter Seven

Agapanthus and Major Bark
whizzed into the kitchen,
making so much noise
that good little Mommy
and good little Daddy
could not understand a word
their girl was saying.

"What happened?" they cried.

"He won! He won!"
yelled Agapanthus,
twirling around like a tornado.
"Major Bark is a champion!"

"Won?" said good little Mommy.

"Won what?" asked good little Daddy.

"A champion blue ribbon!"
Agapanthus shouted.

She stopped twirling
long enough to hug
good little Daddy.
"He got the prize for the dog
with the smallest eyes!" she said.

Good little Mommy
and good little Daddy
put their arms around Agapanthus.

"We are so proud of you,"
good little Mommy said,
"you and your clever bitser."

1st

"Where is he?"
good little Daddy asked.
"Where is this famous ribbon?"

Agapanthus looked around.
Then she got down
on her hands and knees
to see under the table.

"Oh, no!" she squealed.

Major Bark, prize dog
of the smallest eyes
and best animal friend
of Agapanthus Hum,
was chewing his blue ribbon
into a mess of slobber and holes.